A Race to Prayer

Sulaiman's Rewarding Day

By

Aliya Vaughan

THE ISLAMIC FOUNDATION

A Race to Prayer

Published by
THE ISLAMIC FOUNDATION
Markfield Conference Centre, Ratby Lane, Markfield
Leicestershire, LE67 9SY, United Kingdom
E-mail: publications@islamic-foundation.com
Website: www.islamic-foundation.com

Distributed by
KUBE PUBLISHING LTD
T +44 (01530) 249230
info@kubepublishing.com
Website: www.kubepublishing.com

Text © Aliya Vaughan, 2018
Illustrations © Rakaiya Azzouz, 2018
2nd impression, 2020

Book design by Nasir Cadir
Cover design by Sophie Burrows

A Cataloguing-in-Publication Data record for this book is
available from the British Library

ISBN 978-0-86037-653-8
eISBN 978-0-86037-765-8

Contents

Note for parents and teachers   5

A Race to Prayer   7

Evidences from the Qur'an and Sunnah   46

Comprehension questions   48

Inspiration behind the story   50

Glossary   54

The author   56

I pray Allah guides me, you
and all those who read this book
to perform our prayers well.
Ameen.

Note for parents and teachers

Race to Prayer is an exciting story for children about a young Muslim boy who wants to have fun at the quad bike races. Something dramatic happens whereby he learns the importance of praying his prayers on time in their fixed stated times. This is an action most dearest to Allah and worthy of gaining a place in paradise.

Please note that an asterisk* has been used in the text to indicate where Muslims should say a blessing after mentioning the name of the Prophet Muhammad* (peace and blessings be upon him).

Narrated Abdullah bin Masood:
'I asked the Prophet* "Which deed is the dearest to Allah?" He replied, "To offer the prayers at their early stated fixed times..."'
Hadith from the collection of Bukhari

Chapter 1

'Come on!' Sulaiman shouted, punching the air with his fist. 'Put your foot down. They're going to overtake you!'

Huge clouds of sand billowed in the air as the quad bikes roared across the desert terrain. Flashes of colour appeared momentarily before disappearing behind the sand dunes.

His grandpa glanced up from his newspaper and tutted loudly.

'Sulaiman! Stop moving. Every time you move - my paper moves and I cannot read.' He slapped his paper with the back of his hand in annoyance.

Sulaiman quickly shuffled along the sofa so as not to disturb his grandpa. He knew how much he liked to do the crossword in peace. Sulaiman's grandparents were visiting on holiday and he didn't want anything to spoil their trip.

Sulaiman twitched nervously again as he watched the quad bike races live on satellite television. Suddenly the *adhan* interrupted the racing commentary. A picture of the Kaaba with large Arabic writing filled the entire screen. It was time for *Dhuhr*, the mid-day prayer.

'Oh, why did that happen!' Sulaiman huffed. 'Now I'm going to have to go and pray and I'll miss the end of the race.'

'No, you won't,' his grandpa reassured him. 'The races on the television are in Dubai and the time is different over there. We've still got three hours until we have to pray Dhuhr here in Britain.'

Sulaiman was relieved. He knew it was important to perform the five daily prayers at set times throughout the day, but they often clashed with whatever he was doing and he found it hard to steer himself away.

'Anyway you call this racing?' his grandpa continued. 'You haven't seen a proper race until you've seen camels racing. When I was a boy…'

Sulaiman quickly rose to his feet. He could tell Grandpa was going to recall

memories from his childhood. His grandpa was well known for his lengthy stories. Having been raised in the desert with a Bedouin family, he was obsessed with camels. Sulaiman loved his grandpa dearly but he had heard his stories so many times before.

'Er... excuse me, Grandpa,' he interrupted politely. 'I've just remembered I've got to do something.' Before his grandpa could utter another word, Sulaiman had disappeared out of the room.

'Oh!' Grandpa exclaimed, looking baffled. 'Was it something I said?'

Chapter 2

Sulaiman stared at the raindrops as they trickled down his bedroom window. He raced one stream of water against another, his finger pressed firmly on the glass.

'Every time I want to do something exciting, it either rains or it's time to pray,' he moaned.

'Don't complain,' his dad said, watching from the open doorway. 'Rain is a blessing and we are blessed with it quite often here in England.'

'Is it? I don't see how,' Sulaiman replied, throwing himself onto his bed.

'Without rain we wouldn't have drinking water and the trees wouldn't grow and there'd be no crops for us to eat. And

14

without the prayer we might forget to thank Allah for all these blessings.'

Sulaiman grimaced and glanced away. He didn't want to grumble, but it was hard to feel happy when he had nothing to do. His sister, Hannah, had gone to play at her cousin's house and his little brother, Musa, had gone shopping with his mum, leaving him all on his own with no one to play with and nothing to do. His dad smiled and sat down next to him on his bed.

'What did you want to do today?' he asked

'I wanted to play football in the park, but it's raining,' Sulaiman replied, gazing gloomily out of the window. He could see the football pitch in the distance, glinting under a sheen of water. He played there whenever he could, but not today; it was far too wet and muddy.

'I promised I'd take you to the quad bike races in that new stadium just down the road. Why don't we go today?' his dad suggested.

Sulaiman sprang to his feet.

'Oh yes! Yes, please!' he cried.

'Get ready then and I'll ask Grandpa if he wants to join us.'

As his dad left the bedroom, Sulaiman frantically tugged at his pyjamas to change into some clean clothes. His green trousers clashed with his orange sweatshirt, but he was too excited to notice.

'Don't forget to do wudu before we leave,' his dad reminded him. 'We may not have time while we're out.'

Sulaiman dashed into the bathroom

and locked the door.

'And remember to brush your teeth,' his dad shouted through the key hole.

After washing in the bathroom Sulaiman hurried to the front door to put on his trainers. As he tied his laces, his grandma handed him a small, black knapsack.

'Here's your packed lunch. Hurry now, your dad and grandpa are waiting for you in the car. Have fun.'

'Thank you, Grandma.' Sulaiman beamed. He took the bag, kissed his grandmother on her cheek and bounded out the front door.

'Sulaiman! Come back!' she called.

He glanced back to see his grandma waving his coat from the open doorway.

'It's raining! You'll get wet if you don't wear your coat,' she reminded him.

'Thank you. As-salamu alaykum,' Sulaiman replied, his voice echoing through the corridor and down the stairwell. His grandma's reply was drowned out by his quick footsteps, as he ran down the stairs and out through the main door.

Chapter 3

The car was parked on the street where Sulaiman lived. His dad had left the door open so Sulaiman could quickly jump in out of the rain. He slid across the back seat and settled into his position behind Grandpa. He clicked the seatbelt into the fastener and waited eagerly for his dad to start up the engine.

Whirr…chug…chug! Splutter! Splutter!
BANG! His dad froze. Smiling nervously at Grandpa, he made another attempt to start the car. There was a dull, clicking sound as he turned the ignition key. He made a third attempt, but still nothing happened.

'I don't think we'll be going anywhere today,' Grandpa said. 'It was probably never meant to be.'

Tears welled up in Sulaiman's eyes and he slumped down into his seat.

'First it was the rain and now THIS!'

'Let's not give up just yet,' his dad chirped. He pulled a lever under the dashboard to release the safety catch on the car bonnet.

'It's probably a spark plug or something,' his dad muttered as he got out of the car.

He disappeared behind the raised bonnet to inspect the engine. Sulaiman and Grandpa waited patiently in the car until he had finished. Sulaiman was used to his dad tinkering around, mending things, like the time Dad fixed his kite after it got snagged on the branch of a tree.

'Let's try again, shall we?' Rainwater dripped from his dad's curly, black hair and off the end of his nose. He grabbed an old rag from the glove compartment and wiped his face. He then wiped the grease from his hands and turned the ignition key once more. Still nothing happened. Sulaiman's anticipation turned to disappointment.

'Pity we haven't got a camel,' grandpa said. His eyes glazed over as he remembered his beloved childhood pet. 'You can always rely on a camel!'

'Not to worry,' said Dad. 'We can take the bus instead. The stadium is only down the road.'

Sulaiman had been sure his dad would find a solution. He grabbed his knapsack, leapt out of the car and ran briskly with his dad and grandpa to the nearest bus stop.

Chapter 4

Sulaiman huddled under the bus shelter with his dad and grandpa to keep dry from the heavy rain.

His grandpa always wore his traditional Arab dress, but because it was winter it was hidden under a long, thick overcoat. Only a hint of white material could be seen poking out underneath. While they

were waiting, his dad searched his pockets for some loose change for the bus fare.

'Does anyone want a toffee?' he asked, holding a few small sweets in his open hand.

'Not for me. It might pull my false teeth out!' said Grandpa, winking. Sulaiman sniggered and took one of the sweets from his dad. He tore off the wrapper and popped it into his mouth.

'Haw lom do we haff to waay?' Sulaiman mumbled as his tongue lolloped over the chewy candy.

'What did you say?' his dad asked, raising an eyebrow. Sulaiman pushed the sweet to one side. His cheek bulged like a hamster hoarding a mouthful of food.

'I said, how long do we have to wait?'

'Not long. Here comes one now!'

A red, double-decker bus was approaching. It slowed and pulled up to the curb with an abrupt stop. Air hissed as the double doors swung open. They quickly boarded, paid their fare and sat down at the back of the bus. After several stops they reached the stadium. Sulaiman noticed a long queue of people waiting outside the entrance.

'Will we be able to get in, Dad?' he asked anxiously.

'I hope so. We don't want to get wet from the rain, do we?'

They stood in line and slowly shuffled forward as each person bought their ticket.

When it was finally their turn, Dad paid for three tickets. They were each given a stripy green wristband to wear.

They slipped them on and pushed their way through the turnstiles. As they walked down a narrow alleyway towards the arena, they could hear the roar of the quad bikes rumbling louder and louder. Once inside, they saw a giant sandy racetrack with slopes and uneven mounds. A line of thick rubber tyres separated the spectators from the track. They searched for their seat numbers and sat down.

The races were about to begin.

Chapter 5

The quad bikes were all lined up at the starting position. The riders wore coloured helmets, padded leather suits and sturdy black boots. Plumes of grey smoke billowed from exhaust pipes as they revved their engines. A man's voice boomed over the loudspeakers and echoed around the stadium.

'Welcome ladies and gentleman! I'm your commentator for today. We hope you will enjoy the spectacular races we have lined up for you this afternoon.'

After working the crowd into a frenzy, the commentator introduced the names and numbers of each rider, describing the model and make of their quad bike.

'Bobby Biker is rider number nine. He's riding a red quad bike with flashy, gold tyre rims.'

'That one's mine!' Sulaiman shouted, eager to choose his favourite before someone beat him to it. Dad and Grandpa quickly selected their favourite rider.

Suddenly the starter gun fired and the quad bikes roared off. The atmosphere in the stadium was electric. All the spectators stood up in their seats, shouting and waving for the riders to go faster. A man in a seat behind them sounded a few blasts on his gas canister horn. Sulaiman winced and covered his ears with his hands.

'Arrrh! That was loud!' he shouted.

'I'm glad I'm a bit deaf,' Grandpa laughed.

The quad bikes thundered past along the track, the riders standing up in their saddles to soften the impact over the humps. They swerved quickly to the left, then to the right, hugging the bend tightly on the inside lane. They raced around the track three times until they approached the home straight and the finishing line.

'And the winner is…number four!' the commentator announced.

'Yes! My bike won!' Grandpa bellowed.

'You may have won this time, Grandpa,

but I'll win the next race,' Sulaiman growled, flashing a toothy competitive grin.

The riders lined their bikes into position again. The starter gun fired and they sped away, leaving a trail of smoke lingering in the air behind them. After several laps they were all jostling for first place.

'And the winner is…number seven!' the commentator announced, sounding even more excited than before the first race.

'I won! I won!' Dad teased. He grabbed Sulaiman's cheeks with both hands and squashed them together. Sulaiman's lips puckered like a cod fish.

Several races passed and Sulaiman still hadn't won, but it didn't matter as he was having too much fun, caught up in the buzz of excitement. He was sure his bike would win soon. Just then the alarm rang out from his dad's mobile phone. It was time for the lunchtime prayer.

'We should find somewhere to pray Dhuhr now,' Dad said.

'But there are still a few more races to go. Why don't we pray when they stop for a break?' Sulaiman pleaded.

Grandpa remembered how Sulaiman reacted earlier that morning when the *adhan* interrupted the races on T.V.

'The winter prayer times are so close together, it'll be time for the Asr prayer when they stop for a break. We should pray Dhuhr now before it passes,' Grandpa insisted.

Sulaiman didn't want to argue, but he was worried that his bike would win and he wouldn't be there to see it.

'Come on,' Dad encouraged him . 'It won't take long. Allah will reward us more if we do it now.'

Chapter 6

They shuffled past the spectators and made their way up the steps leading out of the arena. Sulaiman trailed reluctantly behind them.

'We could have waited until the break,' he muttered. They walked through the corridors, searching for an attendant to ask where to pray.

'You can go in here,' said a bubbly, young guide who led them down a passageway to a little side room.

'Has everyone got wudu?' Dad asked.

Sulaiman and Grandpa both nodded. They then stood side by side in a straight line as Sulaiman's dad led them in the prayer.

When they had finished, they walked back through the corridors to the arena. As they approached the steps, they noticed the races had stopped. A section of spectator seats had been evacuated and people were standing in the aisles. As they got nearer, they could see part of the ceiling had caved in. Water was dripping from a hole where the roof had been. A security guard held out his hand to prevent them from getting any closer.

'Sorry, I can't let you through,' he said. 'We've had to block this area off.'

Sulaiman stood on the tips of his toes and peered around the security guard to get a better look. He gasped.

'Subhanallah! The roof fell on our seats!'

He turned to see his dad and grandpa. They were visibly shocked. His grandpa swayed and stumbled backwards. He grabbed a handrail and sat down in an empty seat. The band on his head scarf slipped forward and rested awkwardly on the bridge of his nose.

'Are you alright?' Sulaiman asked, placing his hand on his grandpa's shoulder. Grandpa just stared, mouth open wide at the scene.

'Was anybody hurt?' Dad asked.

'A man suffered a few minor injuries,' the security guard replied. 'He's being treated in the first-aid room. It's a good job no one was sitting next to him though; they would have been seriously hurt.'

'Yes, alhamdulillah!' Dad sighed with relief. 'It's just as well we went to pray at the time we did, otherwise that roof would have hit us!'

'Our prayers literally saved us!' Sulaiman cried.

Grandpa was still lost for words. The security guard moved to the front of the crowd and spoke through a microphone.

'The riders are going to stop for a break now,' he announced. 'It'll give us time to clear up this mess and make the area safe again. There's a cafeteria on the second floor if you want to get something to eat and drink. If you come back at half past two, we should know if it's safe to continue the races.'

Sulaiman suddenly remembered the bag his grandma had packed for them that morning.

'We can eat our packed lunch in the cafeteria, can't we, Dad?'

Dad nodded and helped Grandpa stand back up on his feet.

'I think Grandpa needs a cup of tea too… to recover from the shock of it all.'

Chapter 7

While they were eating lunch in the cafeteria, Dad reminded Sulaiman of the importance of performing the prayers at their earliest, fixed times.

'It's easy to get distracted when you're enjoying yourself,' Dad admitted. 'But we shouldn't delay our prayers. We can always come back to our work or play afterwards.'

Grandpa nodded and sipped his tea.

'If we didn't pray when we did, we could have been hurt and spent the afternoon in hospital. Then we would have missed *all* the races.' Sulaiman thought for a moment as he delved his spoon into his raspberry yoghurt.

'This reminds me of Prophet Sulaiman*. He missed the Asr prayer because he was distracted by his beautiful horses.'

'Yes, and Allah will test **us** with **our** prayers just as He tested Prophet Sulaiman*,' said Dad. 'Nothing should be more important than our prayer. The first thing we shall be asked about on the Day of Judgement is our prayers, so we should make sure we perform them on time.'

Sulaiman reflected on his dad's words.

'It must be time for the Asr prayer now, isn't it?' he asked. His dad checked the time on his phone.

'Yes. It's coming up any minute now.'

They gathered their belongings and searched for the little side room to pray again. After they performed Asr, Sulaiman's dad checked the time once more.

'It's nearly half past two. Let's go back to the races now.'

As they were entering the arena, the security guard stopped them again.

'I'm sorry, I can't let you in,' he said. 'We've had to close this section for safety reasons.'

Sulaiman groaned with disappointment.

'Never mind,' his dad comforted him. 'We can come back again another day.'

'No! You don't understand,' said the security guard 'You can still watch the races, but you can't sit here, it's too dangerous. We've moved you to some other seats just over there.'

He pointed to the front row with the aerial of his two-way radio.

'Oh subhanallah!' Sulaiman exclaimed. 'We can see even better from down there. Come on Dad, quickly, they're about to begin the next race!'

Sulaiman bounded down the steps towards their new seats. His dad and grandpa followed quickly behind him. The riders revved their engines in preparation for the new round of races. A strong smell of petrol and smoke lingered in the air. Sulaiman's dad cupped his hand around Sulaiman's ear so he could be heard above the noise of the bikes.

'It looks as though Allah has already rewarded you for doing your prayers,' he said in a raised voice. Sulaiman smiled and nodded.

'Do you think Allah will reward me some more and make my bike win the next race?' he asked excitedly.

'Let's see, shall we,' his dad laughed. 'Let's see.'

Evidences from the Qur'an and Sunnah

In Islam, the prayer is very important and unlike any other act of worship. It is the first action we will be asked about on the Day of Judgment. The Prophet* said:

'The first thing about which the people will be called to account out of their actions on the Day of Judgment is

prayer.... If it is perfect, that will be recorded perfect.'

Narrated by Abu Hurayrah.

Hadith from the collection of Abu Dawood.

If our prayers are performed well they can be a way to enter Paradise. Allah says in the Qur'an:

'Those who humble themselves in their prayers... And who (strictly) guard their prayers; – these will be the heirs, Who will inherit Paradise: they will dwell therein (for ever).'

Surah Al-Mu'minun (The Believers) 23:2,9-11

Comprehension questions

1. What was Sulaiman doing when Grandpa was reading his newspaper?

2. What stopped Sulaiman playing football in the park? What are the blessings of this usually?

3. What did Sulaiman's dad promise to do one day with Sulaiman?

4. As Sulaiman was getting changed out of his pyjamas what did his dad tell him to do?

5. What happened to the car and what did they do instead?

6. Grandpa refused something as he thought it would pull his false teeth out. What was it?

7. What did the alarm on his dad's mobile signal it was time for?

8. Why was Sulaiman upset about leaving to pray while the quad bikes were still racing?

9. What happened when they returned to their seats in the stadium?

10. Which prophet was distracted from doing the Asr prayer by his beautiful horses?

11. What is the first thing Allah will ask us about on the Day of Judgement?

12. What was Sulaiman rewarded with when he returned to the stadium after doing his prayers?

Inspiration behind the story

This story was inspired by an incident that occurred in 1980 when my husband was watching a football match in the capital city of Algeria, Algiers. When the *adhan* for the dhuhr prayer was called, my husband left the spectator seats to perform the prayer. It was while he was praying that an earthquake measuring

7.3 on the Richter scale occurred. It is reported that 3,500 people died and many buildings were destroyed making 300,000 people homeless. For the praying people, Allah took their lives while they were performing an obligatory act of worship. For the people who were not praying on time, Allah took their lives while they were doing other activities. For the people who survived and were left homeless, all they had left were their prayers to ask Allah for help.

You'll be pleased to know my husband survived, as too did all the other spectators in the stadium.

No matter what we are doing, we should organise our lives around the prayer times, and not try to fit the prayers around our activities. The prayer doesn't take long to perform and is much more important than work or play. Allah can make anything happen when we least expect it, so let's make sure we pray on time.

Glossary

Adhan – call to prayer.

Alhamdulilah – this phrase means 'all praise and thanks be to Allah' in English.

Ameen – means 'O Allah, respond to (or answer) what has been said.' If someone says '*Ameen*', it is as if he made the du'a (prayer) to Allah to accept and respond to what was said.

As-salamu alaykum – is the Islamic Arabic greeting. It means 'peace be upon you' in English.

Asr – the third of the five daily prayers, also known as the late afternoon prayer.

Dhuhr – the second of the five daily prayers. Also known as the mid-day prayer.

Kaaba – a large cube-shaped building inside the al-Masjid al-Haram mosque in Mecca.

Subhanallah – is an Arabic phrase meaning 'Glory be to Allah' in English.

Wudu – the ritual washing performed by Muslims before prayer. Also known as ablution in English.

The author

Alison Vaughan is an English revert to Islam. She has had a passion for writing since winning a writing competition at school aged 10 years old. During her teenage years, pen pals across the world enjoyed receiving her lengthy, descriptive letters and later on, her university friends enjoyed the same. She developed her love of writing children's stories whilst home educating her children. It was a creative, fun and engaging way for her children to learn through story-telling. In 2008 Alison won *Best Children's Story* and *Writer of the Year* at the Muslim Writers Awards under her Muslim name, Aliya.